OUR MISERABLE LIFE

WILLIAM STEIG

Our Miserable Life

With a Foreword by Albert Hubbell

THE NOONDAY PRESS
MICHAEL DI CAPUA BOOKS
FARRAR, STRAUS AND GIROUX *New York*

FOREWORD

IT HAS BEEN more than fifty years since William Steig's first book of drawings, called *About People*, introduced us to a new way of regarding our fellow human beings. Now, as this most awful of all centuries slouches toward the year 2000, comes the twelfth successor to that volume, entitled *Our Miserable Life*, a collection of drawings which includes a motley of God's creatures—men, women, dogs, cats, birds—in various dilemmas, predicaments, and vexed straits, and which, on the whole, bears out the title's suggestion that life is more a crock than it's a bowl of cherries. Some of the troubles afflicting these persons are obscure, although all are obviously of a grave nature, and yet we laugh when we look at them, for Steig is a comic artist in the same sense that Charlie Chaplin was. Chaplin could show us naked despair, and the death of hope in the little people of this world, and leave us strangling with laughter even as our hearts went out in sympathy. So Steig, who never ridicules his people, and who has no meanness in him, makes us laugh at their condition, because we know that but for the (temporary) grace of someone or other, we could be in the same fix, and when things get that bad, laughter is the only reasonable response.

I cannot imagine anything more rash or more doomed to fail than an attempt to interpret Steig's drawings psychoanalytically. Pulling a long face and reading eschatological or other meanings into them would be equally foolish. This is graphic art, and graphic art is best dealt with on its own terms—lines and hatchings and smears and smudges put down on paper to convey a thought about something, or just to create a drawing, like Steig's of a rainy day, for its own sweet sake. A Steig drawing is not an illustration to illuminate a situation or an idea; it *is* the idea.

Instead of any gratuitous exegesis, then, I will set down a few thoughts that have been stimulated by these drawings.

Put it down to fancifulness if you will, but I believe you can *hear* some of these drawings: sounds, just barely sub-audible to be sure, seem to come from them, the way they seem to come from some of Goya's etchings and the fearful drawings of Urs Graf. You can hear the silly little noises coming from the demented professorial type sitting beside his sleeping cat, the faint twittery screeching floating above the heads of the three creatures in "Spectators," the wisps of faint keening emanating from the unrequited spinster in "Someday he'll come along . . . ," the rasp and snarl of the heavy pen lines in "Armistice." Perhaps you don't go along with me on this; if not, it's all right.

Steig's people can be energetic, even violently so, but they don't appear to be in very good health, and some are in a very bad way, physically speaking. Think of what must be the severe visceral dislocations in the abdomen of the man in the flowery chair in "Intransigent" to account for his fierce dyspeptic expression, and his all too easily imagined politics, or ponder the mental health of the two cherry-lipped young men who stare vacuously at us in "Sunday." (The man shaving in the Krazy Kat T-shirt doesn't appear to be exactly in the pink, either.) Even so, robust or not, many of these people look as though they could take effective action and are equipped to fulfill their human tasks. James Thurber once decorated the bathroom walls in the apartment of a friend of mine; my friend's landlady was scandalized when she saw the naked men and women chasing and batting at each other in and around the plumbing fixtures in their eternal war, and she told him he'd have to get rid of "those dirty pictures" before he moved. When he told Thurber about it, Thurber said, "My drawings can't be called dirty because my people have no genitals." Well, Steig's drawings are never scabrous either, but not, I daresay, for that reason; most of these men and women seem to be quite susceptible to the power of love and lust, and capable of vigorously responding to it. The intentions of the concupiscent gentleman ogling the plaster bust of a toothsome dame in a window display are surely not innocent (although what he has in mind, considering that the lady ends just below the rib cage, remains a puzzle). The man in proud possession of the large nude female recumbent at his feet in the drawing titled "Estate" surely knows the value of what he has, and what to do with it. In a more outré context, who can doubt the sexual proclivities of the doglike creature with the head of the Emperor Louis-Napoléon who lies in front of the chaise longue on which his mistress voluptuously reclines; how account, otherwise, for her blissful smile of satisfaction?

I like the tantalizing little fragments and hints of drama we are treated to in this book. Why is that middle-aged virago in "Grievances" so pissed off at the sun? What sad denouement lies ahead for the booby son of the farm couple who, mounted on his bicycle, is about to leave home to seek his fortune in "The Son Sets Out for the Big City"? There is something chilling and sinister in the little drawing of the man carrying a swooning woman into a dark wood ("The Other Man's Wife"). And then there is the deceptively peaceful scene in which a man, his pipe in his mouth and wearing a smile of contentment, lies floating on his back in the water under a benign sun, all unaware of the dastardly submarine attack about to be made on his underside by a fearfully fanged aquatic beast that can only be a Steigosaurus.

But enough. I would apologize for detaining you from the enjoyment of these wonderful drawings were it not for the suspicion that you looked at all of them before reading this foreword.

Albert Hubbell

FOR JEANNE

The Napper Wakes

Traveling Companions

Someday he'll come along . . .

Man Answering a Questionnaire

Love's Old Sweet Song

Let's All Be Friends

Cha Cha Cha

Memories

Ideal Woman

Man and Nature

Memory Lane

Insomnia

Evening Alone

The Conversation Takes a Nasty Turn

Rift

The Awakening

Bashful Suitor

Roadblock

The Four of Us
Central Park

W. Steig

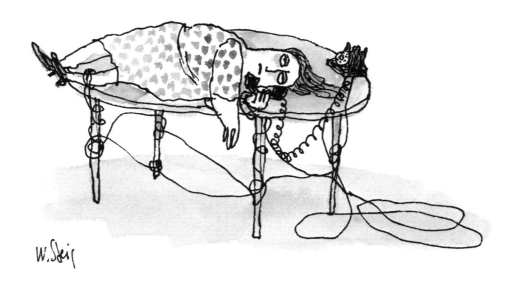

Long Story

Estate

Lovesick Maidens

Social Club

Cha Cha Cha

Showdown

The Son Sets Out for the Big City

Island

Why so pale and wan, fond lover?

Jilted Lover

Who was that lady I seen you with last night?

The Blues

Indecent Proposal

Family

Coward

Wound

Cha Cha Cha

Another Spring

Brothers

Despair

Grievances

Wandering Minstrel

Posse

He's Waiting for His Date to Finish Dressing

Pocket Knife

Playland

The Consolation of Philosophy

Birthday

Intransigent

All Is One

Cha Cha Cha

Phobia

Broken Blossom

Inklings of Eternity

Leaderless Group

A Long Way from Home

Origin of the Species

Spectators

Civil Disobedience

Rush Hour

Conquest of Nature

Parting of the Ways

Cha Cha Cha

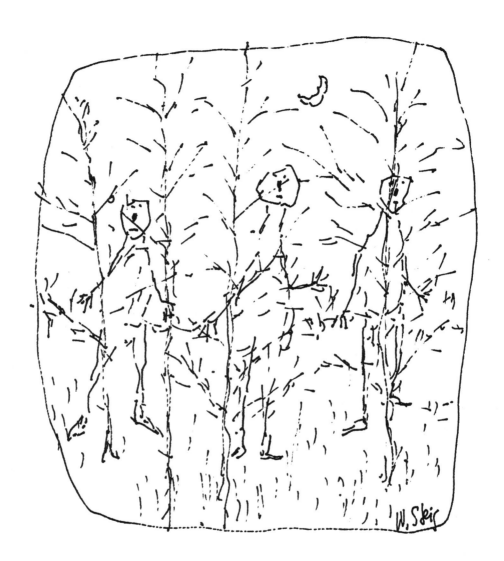

New Moon

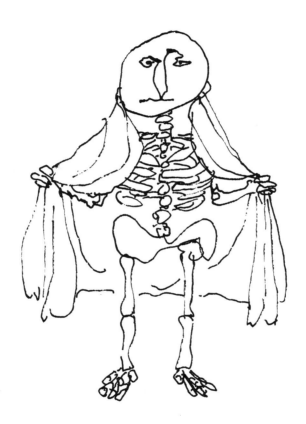

The Way It Is

He Remembers His Childhood

Fate

Birdsong

Penitent

Armistice

Rush Hour

Prep School

Sunday

Bad Lad, Sad Dad

From an Album

Stage Fright

Motherless Child

Unaccountable Sadness

Birdland Revisited

Bonding

The Clamor of Birds

A Book, a Pet, a Box of Bonbons

W.Step

The Mill of the Mind

Cha Cha Cha

Dirt

The Ancient Curse

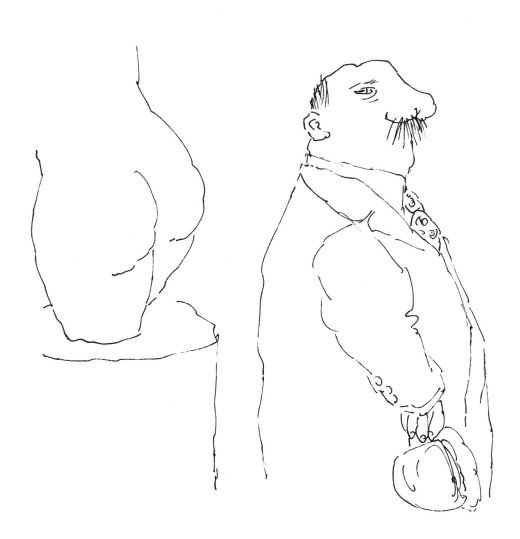

The Other Man's Wife

Outing

Late Bloomer

Passing Through

Respite

So Much to Do

Cha Cha Cha